THE PEBBLETONS

Pebbles on a Mission!

Katy Paddenburg

For my small but mighty pebbles
Bella and **Raffy**

never stop dreaming,
imagining, creating
and loving.

For the rock to my world **Paul**.

Down on the beach and under the pier way down near Padykin Docks, live a bunch of friendly ever so polite, cute and curious rocks.

They are the Pebbletons of Padykin Bay, and as their name suggests, are Pebbles but with great **BIG** ideas that with you they wish to address.

Paddy, Pippy, Paul and Peg and not forgetting dear little Pearl, are proud and loud and full of ideas for our ever so wonderful world.

You see they believe that each of us, regardless of our size, has the chance to make a change by finding inspiration inside.

If we stop . . . take a moment . . . and go outside
and breathe, then we become inspired by the
things we can achieve.

Not for ourselves but for our planet, as it's good to think of others. Especially our beautiful World full of land, earth, sea and vibrant colours.

Now here is a tale of how this super troop one day came to be, one sunny afternoon whilst taking tea beside the sea.

A wave crashed in and shrieked in fear for in its frothy foam, was a baby seagull trapped in litter and far away from home.

Pippy dropped his cuppa' tea and jumped up to lend a hand. Whilst Pearl cried and shouted "I just don't understand!

"How did this baby seagull (who we later know as Dave), arrive in such peril and all covered in mayonnaise?!

"Yes, I agree it's for eating and a good condiment without a doubt, but we need to lend a hand and help this poor baby out."

"CHIPS! CHIPS!" the seagull squawked, unaware of his own fate. There was no time to finish their tea, they knew this couldn't wait!

The Pebbletons assembled and headed down
to the shoreline.

It was a slow-motion scene of five heroes glowing in the sunshine.

"Here's the plan of action!" Paul drew a sketch upon the sand, Paddy and Peg were instructed to pull the baby gull to land.

Whilst Pippy sang sea shanties to calm baby Dave down, Pearl and Paul were to unwrap him from the litter so he wouldn't drown!

The master plan sprang into action, and everyone had their jobs. An awesome team of pebbles, a spontaneous flash-mob.

Dave was a little dizzy from being tangled up for so long. It took all their mighty effort and even a little song.

A-pulling and a-pushing, uncoiling plastic wrapped around his chest, they freed the baby seagull and had succeeded in their quest.

They felt totally chuffed to bits and high-fived in the delight, for they had been inspired to save Dave from his perilous plight.

Dave's mum circled round and landed with an almighty **CRASH!** She'd had a bird's eye view and seen Dave splish and splash.

But she was unable to help – "I just don't have arms and legs!" Then five heroes came along . . . "It's okay, you can call me Peg."

"Peg, thank you and to all of you for helping Dave with this deed. I'm in massive debt to you, is there anything you need?"

"Well, this gives me a thought," said Paddy
who was sipping on cold tea,
"We should set up a super cool squad for
helping others right here beside the sea."

"Yes!" squawked Doris (that's Dave's Mum),
"I would very much like to join the crew."
"The more the merrier!" exclaimed Pearl.
"That's exactly what we will do!"

"Maybe we should look at litter, tidy the beach
and keep it clean. Then there's the planet, let's
plant more trees and strive to keep it green."

"Well, I've got these new funky shoes,"
said Paul, "and I'd like to show them off.
What about inspiring others to walk?"
"Ahem, can I join?" Peg said with a little cough.

"I've always wanted jazzy shoes to parade
the promenade."
"A wonderful message," said Doris,
"and it wouldn't be that hard!

"Those things called cars pollute the air and
my asthma flares up bad.
Plus, I read in the paper it's not good for our
planet and that makes me feel quite sad."

"It's agreed! We are The Pebbletons," said Pippy, "Pebbles on a mission. Everyone is free to join, there are no limits or conditions.

"We'll all choose a super mission that is closest to our heart and strive to look after our planet and today's the day it starts!"

They all proposed a toast with sea-foam mocktails and seaweed treats, for a successful day saving young Dave was no small feat.

"CHIPS!", squawked baby Dave the gull and everyone just laughed.
"Yes," said Doris ". . . you must be hungry after today and that unexpected bath.

"I will get you some nice fresh chips after your brave escapade, although perhaps this time round you will eat them without mayonnaise!?"

They all laughed and cheered in jest –
a happy friendly team, inspired to help our
planet and living the heroes' dream.

THE HEROES

Paddy likes to champion the planting of many trees, which – did you know? - have magical powers that help the planet to breathe.

These magical beings made up of roots, trunks, branches, shoots and leaves give us fresh clean air to consume, take in and breathe.

Planted is the name of Paddy's charity . . . the mission: to plant lots of trees inland or beside the sea.

He pops on his oversize boots and picks up a pack of seeds, then sprinkles them with hope and love as that's just what our planet needs.

OF OUR STORY

Pippy is a litter picker and takes great pride in performing this, picking up rubbish where the bin has sadly been missed.

Litter can be dangerous for our furry and feathered mates, so, help them out and tidy up as there is literally no time to waste!

After a day at school, Pippy gathers up some friends to head down to the beach before the sun goes down and the day comes to an end.

Gloves and sticks in hand they pick up any waste they see whilst chanting sea shanties, of course, as happy as can be.

Paul and **Peg** are a dream team and think more towards the air. Their mission is a simple one . . . they walk everywhere!

They could have bought a Pebblemobile, but why would they do that?
Such machines pollute the air and walking is better for you . . . that's a FACT!

For walking, Peg bought some jazzy shoes and Paul some Nordic walking sticks. They mooch along like the coolest pair inspiring other pebbles to keep fit.

Fitness, and the fact we can walk, bus or bike will help the atmosphere. So, pop on your jazziest shoes and join these funky pioneers.

Little **Pearl**, the smallest of pebbles but mighty big in plans, has set up a recycling pod for paper, plastic, glass, and cans.

If we are mindful and separate before throwing things away, we help our planet, animals and ourselves. That deserves a GIANT hip hip hooray!

Pearl has also set up three boxes in the house beside the bin, Blue for paper, green for glass, yellow plastic, cans and tins.

Pearl likes to be organised that's for sure, but behind everything that's done is a want to help planet Earth and Pearl believes this is a mission for everyone.

So now you've met the Pebbletons,
from Paddy to dear little Pearl.
All loud and proud and full of ideas for
our unique and wonderful World.

BE INSPIRED . . . . .

They truly believe that each of us, regardless of our size, has the chance to help our planet so become inspired and get outside!

BE MORE PEBBLE!

Printed in Great Britain
by Amazon